THE SCORCH TRIALS

(The Maze Runner, book 2)

SIDEKICK
to the novel

by

MIRIAM SOKOLOW

Published by

WeLoveNovels

Disclaimer: This publication is an unofficial Sidekick to *The Scorch Trials* and does not contain the novel. It is designed for fiction enthusiasts who are reading the novel, or have just finished. Order a copy of the novel *The Scorch Trials* on Amazon.

WeLoveNovels maintains an independent voice in delivering critical analysis and commentary; we are not affiliated with or endorsed by the publisher or author of *The Scorch Trials*.

Questions? Ideas? Comments?

Email founders@welovenovels.com.

We are listening!

IV

marked.) You can order a copy of the novel on Amazon.

* * *

Disclaimer: I'm not James Dashner. I don't know James Dashner. Neither I nor WeLoveNovels has any association with James Dashner whatsoever. What you've got in your hands is 100% independent and unauthorized opinion, commentary, and analysis.

The Scorch Trials
A Sidekick to the James Dashner Novel

Chapters 8-14

The Rat Man tells the Gladers that upon completing the Scorch Trials they will be given the cure for the Flare illness. If there is a cure, why put the Gladers through the Trials? The Rat Man says that the cure is so expensive few can afford it. If WICKED has indeed been granted "nearly unlimited money" by the world governments, why don't they simply manufacture enough of the cure to fix everyone? It's a good guess that either the cure the Rat Man promises is a fiction, or the catastrophe WICKED hopes to stave off is separate from the illness.

Much of Thomas's internal character struggle in the previous book revolved around learning to trust the other Gladers. With the Rat Man's revelation about the illusions ("Sometimes what you see is not real, and sometimes what you do *not* see *is* real"), the Gladers find their own senses being used against them. Forget about trusting Aris—can Thomas even trust himself and what he sees? For all they know, the Gladers could be running around a large, empty room, caught up in a mental Matrix.

Chapter 15-22

Winston's burns foreshadow the sunburned plain the Gladers encounter above the stairs. The silver ball pools from the ceiling before attacking and burning Winston, much like the solar flares lashed out at Earth. Both attacks are unprovoked, unexpected, and unavoidable. WICKED, however, seems far more malevolent than the solar flare. Unlike a natural catastrophe, it intentionally causes the Gladers harm. However, also unlike a natural disaster, WICKED has a supposedly noble goal in mind, raising the age-old philosophical question of whether the ends justify the means. If the suffering of the Gladers will save millions of lives, then is it "worth it"? The Gladers feel animosity towards WICKED even after learning of the purpose for the Trials; after all, they never signed up for any of this. However, they also espouse this philosophy at times. While Thomas tries to save other Gladers, his primary goal is preserving his own life. When other Gladers are killed along the way, he sees it as unfortunate but not debilitating. The other Gladers are willing to sacrifice a few in order to preserve themselves—think about the moment when Thomas, Minho, and Newt leave the stairwell first. In other words, their personal ends justify the means.

did WICKED invent the Flare itself? The solar flare scorches the Earth with devastating effect, which makes sense. But this strange virus caused by the flare, on the other hand, does not.

Chapters 39-46

WICKED pulls Thomas out of the Scorch Trials to heal his gunshot wound and resultant infection, citing him as one of four or five important Candidates. It's a strange occurrence, since WICKED has no problem tossing Thomas into deadly situations. They imply that the Trials' purpose is to gather specific brainwaves in the Gladers' minds. Since the Flare exists in the mind, WICKED must be hoping that certain brain patterns can eradicate the virus. This means that the promised cure is still a fiction—or that by completing the Scorch Trials, the Gladers will create the proper brain patterns and therefore manufacture the cure themselves.

Harriet is likely named after Harriet Tubman, the famous abolitionist, although there are several famous scientists with that name who could also be the source. Sonya may be named after Sofia Kovalevskaya, a brilliant mathematician who later changed her name to Sonya.

Group B must kill Thomas in order to beat their Scorch Trial. There are maybe twenty-five girls remaining, far more than the ten boys Thomas left behind. From a purely utilitarian perspective (and Thomas's willingness to let others die for the sake of

WICKED could create visual illusions, but his words are illusions too, filled with lies and false promises.

Throughout the book, Thomas has leaned further and further towards the idea that the ends justify the means, if only when it suits his own purposes. WICKED, strangely, seems more altruistic; the initial Creators worked to create a better future they would not live to see, albeit built on the suffering of over a hundred children.

The Scorch Trials
A Sidekick to the James Dashner Novel

Although Teresa is subjected to similar difficulties as Thomas during the Trials and is forced to destroy her relationship with him, she retains faith that WICKED is ultimately working for the good and their sacrifices are necessary for humanity's survival. Teresa is more altruistic than Thomas, and more willing to see the good in others. She quickly sees that Brenda is vying for Thomas's affections, but helps pull Brenda back on board the Berg without hesitation. Teresa's sacrifices take a heavy toll on her, but her refusal to continuously apologize for her fake betrayal indicates great inner strength.

Minho

In *The Maze Runner*, Minho was a Runner, a prestigious group of Gladers who ran sections of the Maze every day, mapping it out. Although Minho was the head Runner, he offered the position to Thomas after Thomas saved his and Alby's lives. At the start of *The Scorch Trials*, Minho quickly takes control of the Gladers. After WICKED tattoos "The Leader" on Minho's neck, the Gladers officially elect him as their leader.

Minho is initially reluctant to lead the group, but he quickly grows into the role. He keeps the group disciplined and organized, but he also reveals a brutal streak. He physically threatens the other Gladers to keep them in line, and he can be rude and seemingly uncaring. However, Minho proves to be the leader the Gladers need to survive the Scorch. While Thomas is too often sidetracked by his own worries and doubts, especially concerning Teresa, Minho remains focused throughout. When Thomas and Brenda are separated from the group in the Crank town, Minho pursues them. However, when Group B captures Thomas, Minho realizes that because the Gladers are vastly outnumbered, they have no hope of rescuing Thomas, and makes the call to continue on. While the decision to leave his friend behind is not easy, Minho understands that the group's survival matters more than Thomas's. Although unnerved by the "THOMAS IS THE REAL LEADER" signs in the Crank town, Minho continues to support his friend. Minho is practical; he laments Chuck's death primarily because Chuck's cheerfulness was a crucial part of the group dynamic.

The burden of leadership on Minho is increasingly evident throughout the story. Minho did not wish to be leader, and he is uneasy in the position. Nevertheless, he remains an effective and pragmatic leader throughout.

Themes & Symbols You May Have Missed

Illusion

At the beginning of *The Scorch Trials*, WICKED spokesman "the Rat Man" warns the Gladers not to trust anything they see. WICKED's ability to create powerful illusions leaves the Gladers in doubt as to whether the objects they can see, smell, and touch are real. But WICKED's greatest illusions are the ones that involve people, a fact Thomas should have picked up on after learning that the rescuers from the end of *The Maze Runner* were actually part of WICKED. There is little indication of sensory illusions once the Gladers enter the Scorch. Instead, WICKED's illusions come in the form of people. Thomas's greatest challenge comes when Teresa and Aris are forced to lie to Thomas and convince him that their friendship with him, along with Teresa's romantic interest, was a sham in order to save his life. Similarly, Brenda's friendship with Thomas was an illusion.

Without the ability to read minds, no one can be certain that his or her friendships are not illusions, resulting in the need for trust. WICKED's Trials are often designed to be solved and beaten in groups, requiring the Gladers and Group B to work together. Without trust, without the assurance that these friendships are real, the Trials are not survivable. At the end of the novel, Thomas rejects Teresa, saying he cannot trust her anymore. There is strength in numbers. Alone, isolated from his friends, and having rejected the one person capable of communicating with him at a distance, Thomas may be undercutting his own chances for survival.

The Ends Justify the Means

Philosophy 101

The Scorch Trials dips its toes into the murky waters of philosophy to explore the concept of consequentialism. Consequentialism holds that the end goal justifies whatever methods used to reach it—in other words, the ends justify the means. Not discussed is the opposing philosophy of deontology: the methods, not the goal, are what's important. Or, in the words of a common saying, "Life is a journey, not a destination."

In a post-apocalyptic environment, deontology can appear to be a luxury of a time past when survival was not such a struggle. Nevertheless, *The Maze Runner* and *The Scorch Trials* both focus on journeys: first the navigation of the Maze, and then the crossing of the Scorch. By placing the spotlight on the boys' movement from one place to another, Dashner indicates that the journey is important, as are the methods used during it.

Thomas forms close friendships with Newt and Minho over the course of his journey, and these friendships are more important to him personally than saving a world he has no memory of. Teresa's betrayal may have saved his life, which from a consequentialist perspective makes the false betrayal the morally right course of action—but it also severely damages Thomas's relationship with Teresa, leading him to reject her at the end of the novel. Thomas's journey in the Maze and Scorch Trials form and influence his character. There's a reason why Dashner chose not to write the book from the perspective of WICKED; doing so would focus on the destination part of the narrative instead of the Gladers' journey.

In the Final Analysis . . .

The future has never been more uncertain for Thomas than at the end of *The Scorch Trials*. Separated from his friends and voluntarily cut off from Teresa, Thomas waits alone for whatever WICKED has in store for him.

The WICKED scientists' quest to obtain the right brain patterns has led them to subject the Gladers and Group B to experiences designed to invoke terror, fury, hatred, betrayal, and heartbreak. The Gladers and Group B have been repeatedly promised that their suffering will save the world. But if WICKED fails to find a cure, then all the deaths and all the agony will have been for nothing. The burden now lies with WICKED to justify their actions.

Meanwhile, WICKED has remained mum on how they plan to extract these precious patterns from the Gladers' and Group B's brains. Considering the tone of the novels so far, it seems unlikely that the procedure will be benign. Upon regaining their memories, will the Gladers and Group B be asked to donate their brains to science?

Does WICKED's ideology that "the ends justify the means" validate their treatment of the characters thus far? Should "the ends justify the means" have a limit, and if so, where?

So, What'd You Think?

Thanks for investing in this *Sidekick*. Now that you've read it, let us hear from you!

In just a sentence or two, please email founders@welovenovels.com your answer to one simple question:

What was your favorite (or least favorite) thing about this Sidekick?

We want to know what you think, so we can bring you more of what you love most, and fix what you don't like.

And if you would like a free copy of Katherine Miller's top-rated *Sidekick* to *Leaving Time*, Jodi Picoult's latest bestseller, we'd like to send it to you (a $4.99 value). All you have to do is add the words **"Yes, I Want My Bonus Sidekick"** to the email subject line, and you'll get instant access.

The Scorch Trials
A Sidekick to the James Dashner Novel

About the Author of This Sidekick

Miriam Sokolow is a recent college graduate. When not overanalyzing books, she can usually be found playing a mean game of Settlers of Catan or discussing the heteronormative implications of the latest Doctor Who episode.

Other Sidekicks from WeLoveNovels

Sidekick to Go Set a Watchman

Sidekick to The Martian

Sidekick to Luckiest Girl Alive

Sidekick to Seveneves

Sidekick to All the Light We Cannot See

Sidekick to The Nightingale

Sidekick to Wayward

Sidekick to Seveneves

Sidekick to Departure

Sidekick to Orphan Train

Sidekick to Papertowns

Sidekick to Gathering Prey

Sidekick to Pines

Sidekick to Memory Man

Sidekick to The Shadows

Sidekick to The Husband's Secret

Sidekick to A Spool of Blue Thread

Sidekick to The DUFF

Sidekick to Insurgent

Sidekick to Redeployment

Sidekick to The Girl on the Train

Sidekick to Still Alice

Sidekick to Captivated by You

Sidekick to Catching Fire

Sidekick to Mockingjay

Sidekick to Deadline

Sidekick to Big Little Lies

Sidekick to Gone Girl

We are so grateful to all who have taken a moment to leave a quick review of one of our Sidekicks on Amazon. Your thoughtfulness means a

lot and helps us, and the rest of the world, know how
we are doing and how we can improve. :)

Questions? Ideas? Comments?

Email **founders@welovenovels.com**.

We are listening!

The Scorch Trials
A Sidekick to the James Dashner Novel

The Scorch Trials
A Sidekick to the James Dashner Novel

Made in the USA
Las Vegas, NV
13 March 2023